office   Chicago Public Schools

W9-AZM-395

TUTTLE'S SHELL

SALVATORE MURDOCCA

One day George bumped into a great big pumpkin.

He lifted the pumpkin onto his back and started to carry it home.

"Hey," said the pumpkin. "Put me down!"

"I'm sorry, pumpkin," said George.

"I'm not a pumpkin," said the pumpkin.

George looked up. "Tuttle! What are you doing in there?"

"Someone stole my shell while I was taking a bath in the stream," sobbed Tuttle.

"This sounds like the work of Louis," said George.
Tuttle began to cry again.

"Don't cry, Tuttle. I'll help you find your shell," said George.

"What good is that?" asked Tuttle, sniffling. "I can't do anything while I'm in this pumpkin."

George lifted the pumpkin onto his back and started up the road. It was slow going. The pumpkin was very heavy.

Suddenly there was a loud *hssssssssss!* George put down the pumpkin and jumped inside.

Cora looked at the pumpkin and hissed unhappily.

George poked his head out. "I can't play today Cora," he said. "Someone stole Tuttle's shell and we have to find it."

"This sounds like the work of Louis," said Cora.

George slid down the pumpkin and lifted it onto his back. It felt heavier than ever.

"That pumpkin needs some wheels," said Cora.

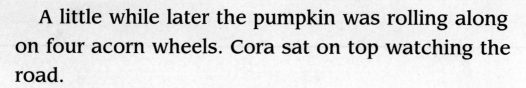

A little while later the pumpkin was rolling along on four acorn wheels. Cora sat on top watching the road.

"ROAD BLOCK!" shouted Cora. But it was too late. They bumped right into a log.

"That log shouldn't be there," said George.

"I like it," said Grouch.

Tuttle poked his head out. "Please move the log," he said. "Someone stole my shell and we're on our way to find it."

Grouch pushed the log off the road. "This sounds like the work of Louis," he grumbled.

George took a deep breath and started pushing the pumpkin.

Grouch shook his head. "You'd better let me help," he said.

So Grouch began to push. Suddenly something flashed by and screeched to a stop.

"W.C. is after me again," said Wilma. "Where can I hide?"

"Get behind the pumpkin!" said George.

W. C. came trotting up. He sniffed the pumpkin.
"What's in there, George?" he asked.

Tuttle poked his head out. "It's me, W. C.," he
said. "Someone stole my shell."

"Sounds like the work of Louis," said W. C.

"That's what we think," said Cora.

W.C. turned to George. "Did you see which way Wilma went?" he asked.

George pointed back down the road.

"Thanks," said W. C. as he trotted off the same way he had come.

Wilma thanked everyone. George and Grouch began to push the pumpkin again.

"Let me help you," said Wilma. "I can pull this pumpkin along pretty fast."

Wilma did go very fast. Everyone hung on tightly to keep from falling off.

The pumpkin screeched around a sharp corner.

"ROAD BLOCK!" shouted Cora. But it was too late.
The pumpkin flipped over.

Leonardo was in the middle of the road, laughing.

"What's so funny?" asked Wilma.

"Louis is up the road dressed like a turtle," said
Leonardo.

"Let's go find him!" said George.

It didn't take long to find Louis. He was admiring his reflection in a pond.

Louis looked up. "Well, well," he said. "Everyone has come to see my new outfit."

"That's my shell!" shouted Tuttle.

"Not any more," said Louis. "Finders keepers, losers weepers."

Tuttle began to weep.

"You must feel very hot in there," said Cora.

"I bet you can't even run in that shell," said Wilma.

Louis ran up the road and back. "I can do anything in this shell," he boasted.

Just then George had an idea. "If we think of something you can't do, will you give Tuttle back his shell?" he asked.

"Sure," said Louis, smiling slyly.

George asked Louis to climb a tree. Louis climbed two. Leonardo asked Louis to swim in the pond. Louis dived right in. It felt good to cool off.

Wilma asked Louis to dig a hole. Louis dug a deep one. He started to feel warm again.

Grouch asked Louis to lift a heavy log. Louis grunted and groaned and lifted the huge log onto his back.

"What are we going to do?" said George.

Tuttle began to smile. "Louis, I'll bet there's one thing you can't do," he said.

"I can do anything," Louis boasted.

"Okay," said Tuttle. "Lie on your back."

Louis let himself fall backwards. "I guess I win," he said.

"Now you have to get up," said Tuttle.

"There's nothing to it," said Louis.

But no matter how hard he tried, Louis simply could not get up. And he was getting very overheated.

"All right," Louis finally gasped. "You win. Just get me out of here!"

Leonardo and George took hold of one arm. Wilma and Cora held the other. Grouch pulled on the shell.

"Hurry! Hurry!" screamed Louis.

The shell was a very tight fit. They pulled and pulled until . . . POP!

Louis was out of the shell. But Grouch and the shell had disappeared.

"Where's my shell?" cried Tuttle.

"Here it is," said Grouch, walking out of the pond.

"Okay, Tuttle," said Louis. "Now let's see if *you* can do it. Let's see you lie on your back and then get up."

Tuttle asked everyone to cover their eyes while he climbed out of the pumpkin and slipped back into his shell.

Tuttle stood up on his hind legs and fell backwards. Then he stretched out his neck and pushed his nose against the ground.

FLOP! Tuttle turned over in a flash.

Everyone clapped except Louis. "I still think that shell looked better on me," he grumbled.

"It's great to be home," said Tuttle.

To my wife Nancy—S.M.

Text copyright © 1999, 1976 by Salvatore Murdocca
Illustrations copyright © 1999 by Salvatore Murdocca

All rights reserved.
No part of this publication may be reproduced, except in the case of quotation for articles or reviews,
or stored in any retrieval system, or transmitted in any form or by any means, electronic, mechanical,
photocopying, recording, or otherwise, without written permission from the publisher.

For information contact:
MONDO Publishing
One Plaza Road, Greenvale, New York 11548
MONDO is a registered trademark of Mondo Publishing
Visit our web site at http://www.mondopub.com
Printed in Hong Kong
99 00 01 02 03 04 05   HC   9 8 7 6 5 4 3 2 1
99 00 01 02 03 04 05   PB   9 8 7 6 5 4 3 2 1

The illustrations were created using gouache, watercolors,
graphite, colored pencils, and water-soluble crayons.
Designed by Mina Greenstein   Production by The Kids at Our House

Library of Congress Cataloging-in-Publication Data
Murdocca, Salvatore.
p.   cm.
Summary· When Tuttle loses his lovely shell to a turtle shell thief, he temporarily uses
a pumpkin while his friends help him search.
ISBN 1-57255-643-9 (hardcover : alk. paper). — ISBN 1-57255-644-7 (paperback : alk. paper)
[1. Turtles—Fiction. 2. Animals—Fiction.] I. Title.
PZ7.M94Tu   1999
[E]—dc21   97-51164   CIP   AC